Little Blossom Stories

The Case of the Wet Pet

By Cecilia Minden

TJ and Mark like to help.

This is Meg and her pet, Jed.

Meg put Jed in the yard.
Now he is wet.

How did Jed get wet?

6   Is there a pond in your yard?

There is not a pond in my yard.

Did Jed get out of your yard?

Jed did not get out of my yard.

That is how Jed got wet!

Turn this off when Jed
is in your yard.

Now Jed will not get wet.

Good work, TJ.
Good work, Mark.

Word List

sight words

a	her	my	pond	to	you
and	How	Now	TJ	Turn	
Good	is	of	the	when	
he	like	off	there	work	
help	Mark	out	This	yard	

short a words	short e words	short i words	short o words	short words
That	Meg	did	not	put
	Jed	in	got	
	wet	will	pond	
	pet			
	get			

TJ and Mark like to help.
This is Meg and her pet, Jed.
Meg put Jed in the yard. Now he is wet.
How did Jed get wet?
Is there a pond in your yard?
There is not a pond in my yard.
Did Jed get out of your yard?
Jed did not get out of my yard.
That is how Jed got wet!
Turn this off when Jed is in your yard.
Now Jed will not get wet.
Good work, TJ. Good work, Mark.

Published in the United States of America by Cherry Lake Publishing
Ann Arbor, Michigan
www.cherrylakepublishing.com

Illustrator: Becky Down

Cherry Blossom Press is an imprint of Cherry Lake Publishing.

Library of Congress Cataloging-in-Publication Data

Names: Minden, Cecilia, author. | Down, Becky, illustrator.
Title: The case of the wet pet / written by: Cecilia Minden ; illustrated by Becky Down.
Description: [Ann Arbor : Cherry Lake Publishing, 2019] | Series: Little blossom stories |
    Summary: "Help TJ and Mark solve the case of the wet pet!"– Provided by publisher. |
    Includes author biography, phonetics, and teaching guide.
Identifiers: LCCN 2019006062| ISBN 9781534149717 (pbk.) |
    ISBN 9781534148284 (pdf) | ISBN 9781534151147 (hosted ebook)
Subjects: | CYAC: Mystery and detective stories.
Classification: LCC PZ7.M6539 Cbw 2019 | DDC [E]–dc23
LC record available at https://lccn.loc.gov/2019006062

Printed in the United States of America
Corporate Graphics

Cecilia Minden is the former director of the Language and Literacy Program at Harvard Graduate School of Education.
She earned her PhD in Reading Education at the University of Virginia. Dr. Minden has written extensively for early reader
She is passionate about matching children to the very book they need to improve their skills and progress to a deeper
understanding of all the wonder books can hold. Dr. Minden and her family live in McKinney, Texas.

CHERRY BLOSSOM PRESS